About the book

Long ago in Russia there lived a cat whose mischievous pranks made him the terror of the village. Finally, his master lost patience with the naughty cat, and he carried poor Catofy deep into the heart of the Cossack forest and left him there all alone.

The animals of the forest had never seen a cat before, and that gave Catofy a fine idea. How Catofy the Clever tricked Missy Fox and Bear and Wolf and earned himself the name of Catofy the Terror makes a wonderfully funny tale that is sure to delight young readers.

Wallace Tripp captures all the whimsical humor of the story in his witty, rollicking drawings. He makes Catofy and Fox, Bear and Wolf unforgettable characters, as lovable as they are funny.

Catofy the Clever,

adapted from a Russian folktale
by
Cynthia Jameson

illustrated by
Wallace Tripp

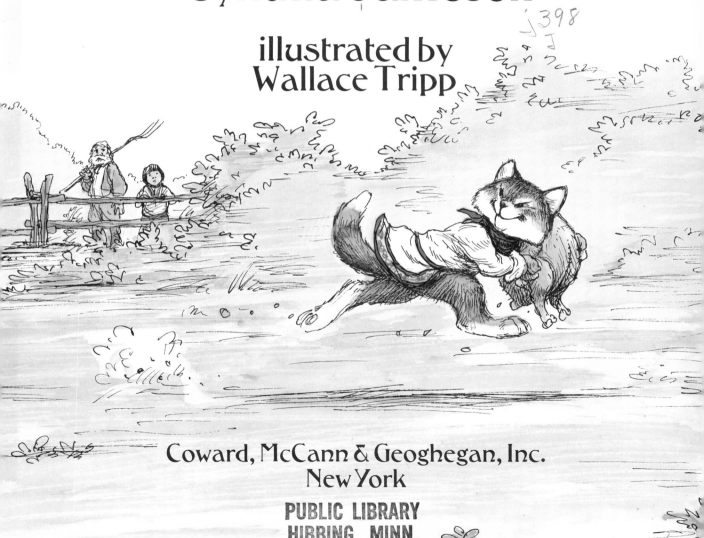

Coward, McCann & Geoghegan, Inc.
New York

Library of Congress Catalog Card Number: 75-169250

Printed in the United States of America

05210

For my mother
Julia Stepanovna

Long ago, in a little Russian village there lived a peasant. Now this peasant had a cat who was the terror of the whole village. Time and again, he would steal whole chickens out of the neighbors' soup kettles. Once he hid out in the dairy shed for two weeks and lapped up all the cream from the village milk buckets.

Before very long, the peasant decided he could take no more of his cat's pranks, so he put him in a sack and carried him off to the Cossack forest. When he reached the darkest depths, he put his burden down and returned home alone.

The poor cat finally chewed a hole in the sack and climbed out. Then he set out to explore the strange forest.

He wandered about for days until he came upon a little hut. He went inside, and found nobody there, so he climbed up to the attic, and made himself a bed in some leaves. He led a carefree life. Whenever he was hungry, he would step outside the door of the hut and catch a few mice or birds. Then, when his belly was full, he would go up to his attic to sleep.

One bright day, while the cat was out walking, he met a fox. Fox took one look at him and exclaimed, "In all the years I've lived in this forest, never have I laid eyes on anything like you!"

Then Missy Fox made a deep curtsy and asked. "Tell me, dear fellow, what on earth are you? How did you find your way here? What might your honored name be?"

The cat bristled with pride and said, "I am Catofy the Clever, who has been sent by the Czar from the Siberian forests to govern you."

"Fancy that!" sighed Fox. "I hadn't heard about you. Come be my guest for supper."

Missy Fox led Catofy the Clever to her den and fed him a platter of delicious roast birds. After supper Missy Fox said, "Tell me, dear boy, have you a wife?"

"No," answered Catofy, "I'm a bachelor."

"Oh, you *are* fortunate!" exclaimed Missy Fox. "I happen to be looking around for a husband myself. Why don't we marry?"

Catofy agreed, and so he and Missy Fox were
married. After the wedding, they prepared a
lavish feast for just the two of them.

The next day, while Catofy slept, Fox set out
to hunt for food. She hunted for hours in
bushes and creeks until she finally caught a fat
wild goose. She was carrying it home to Catofy
when she met Wolf.

"All right, Foxy. Give me that goose!"

"No, I won't!" cried Fox, clutching the goose closer to her.

"Then I'll just have to take it myself," said Wolf.

"If you do, I'll tell Catofy the Clever and he'll have you executed!"

"And just who is your Catofy the Clever?" sneered Wolf.

"Don't tell me you haven't heard! Catofy the Clever has been sent by the Czar from the Siberian forests to govern us. And you are looking at the former Missy Fox, now the honorable and important wife of our new governor, Catofy the Clever."

"Hmmmm," said Wolf, scratching his muzzle. "I'd sure like to get a look at him."

"Well-l-l-l . . . my Catofy is such a devil these days. He's apt to gobble up anyone he doesn't like. But perhaps I can help you get a peek at him. I'll tell you what to do. Go kill a nice fat ram and carry it through the forest to the big red oak. Lay it down under the tree where Catofy will be sure to see it. Then hide yourself in a hurry because if he sees you, you'll never escape with your life."

Wolf hurried off to hunt for a ram, and Fox continued on her way. A little while later she met Black Bear.

"Stay where you are, Missy Fox," said he. "Who's the fat goose for? Hand it over to me!"

"Keep your distance, Black Bear," said Fox, "or else I'll tell Catofy the Clever, and he'll have you executed!"

"Catofy who?" asked Black Bear in surprise.

"Catofy the Clever has been sent by the Czar from the Siberian forests to govern us. I know this because I am Madam Catofy the Clever, honorable and important wife of our new governor." As Fox said this, she puffed out her chest and swished her bushy tail.

"What does he look like?" asked Black Bear, squinting his eyes and looking around. "Will you point him out to me?"

"My word! I wouldn't do a thing like that. He doesn't like to see anyone looking at him. Besides, if you didn't catch his fancy, he'd surely tear you apart and eat you. You'd better do just as I say, and if you're lucky, you'll catch a glimpse of him."

Fox leaned close to Black Bear as if she were about to tell him a secret, and then she began: "You go kill a fat bull and carry it through the forest to the big red oak. When you get there, lay it down under the tree where Catofy will be sure to see it. Make sure you hide yourself as fast as you can, for if he sees you —" But before Fox could finish, Black Bear was already padding off into the forest in search of a fat bull.

In the meantime, Wolf killed a large ram,
carried it through the forest, and laid it down
under the red oak tree. He had just finished
skinning it and was brushing off his coat
when he heard a lot of rustling in the bushes.
He looked up and saw Black Bear slowly crawl-
ing toward the tree with a heavy bull slung
over his shoulders.

"Good day to you, Black Bear," said Wolf.
"Hello, Brother Wolf," panted Black Bear.
"Have you seen Fox and the new governor,
Master Catofy?"

"Not yet," Wolf replied. "But I'm waiting for them myself."

"Why don't you go fetch them while I stand guard here?" suggested Black Bear.

"No, not me!" exclaimed Wolf. "I can't run

as fast as I used to. You'd better go and I'll
wait here."

"Me!" cried Black Bear. "Don't you see how
shaggy and pigeon-toed I am? I could never go
to the governor's house looking the way I do."

Suddenly they heard a splash. Wolf and Black Bear turned and saw Otter paddling lazily along in the creek.

They called out to him, "Hey, Otto! Swim down to Fox's den and tell her we're waiting to have a look at the new governor. And be sure to tell her we've got a nice ram and a fat bull with us here under the big red oak."

And so, while Otter swam as fast as he could to Fox's den, Wolf and Black Bear looked for a good place to hide.

"I'll climb up in the red oak," said Black Bear.
"What?" whined Wolf, who was now beginning to panic. "Where am I going to hide? You know I can't climb trees. Hide me quick — before he comes! Under something. . . ."

Black Bear hid Wolf under some bushes and covered him all over with dried leaves. Then he scrambled up the big red oak — to the very top — and watched to see if Catofy the Clever was coming.

By this time Otter had arrived at Fox's den and told her that Black Bear and Wolf were waiting under the big red oak with a ram and a bull. In no time, Catofy and Fox were on their way to the oak tree.

It was Black Bear who first spotted them from his perch in the tree. He called down to Wolf, in a low voice, "That Catofy certainly is small for a governor!"

Catofy circled the carcasses of the ram and the bull several times. Then he began gnawing and clawing at the meat, growling all the while as if he were angry.

Black Bear whispered down to Wolf, "He may be small, but I see he's got an enormous appetite. That meal would do for ten of us, but I bet it won't be enough for him alone. I hope he doesn't eat us up as well!"

Poor Wolf wanted terribly to get a little look at Catofy the Clever, but he couldn't find a peephole through the leaves. Bit by bit, he cleared some of the dried leaves away from in front of his eyes. But Catofy heard the rustling in the dried leaves! Thinking it was a mouse, he sprang! He sunk his claws and teeth deep into poor Wolf's tender muzzle.

There was a terrible scramble! Wolf howled
more from terror than from pain. He leaped
out of the bushes and ran as fast as he could.

Catofy, frightened to death, clawed his way
up the big red oak where Black Bear was hiding.

"Oh, woe! Oh, woe!" said Black Bear to himself. "He's seen *me* too!"

With a loud crashing and thrashing, Black
Bear slid down the big tree, breaking off every
branch along the way. He crashed to the ground
and was off as fast as his legs could carry him.

Fox, who was watching the whole time, laughed and laughed and shouted after them, "Run faster! Faster! Or he'll get you for sure! Heh, heh, heh...."

It wasn't long before rumors of "Catofy the Terror" spread to every corner of the forest. Animals, large and small, feared him.

Of course, Catofy and Fox had enough meat from the ram and the bull to last them quite a long time. But it's almost all gone now, and you can be sure that the two of them are busily thinking of how they can trick the animals of the forest into bringing them many more fine meals.

About the author

CYNTHIA JAMESON enjoys writing children's stories and poems, especially those about gypsies and animals. When not writing, she spends her time drawing and has done some book illustration.

About the artist

WALLACE TRIPP was born in Boston, Massachusetts. He studied at the University of New Hampshire and was graduated from the Boston Museum School. He has taught both high school and college but now devotes all his time to illustration. CATOFY THE CLEVER is the twenty-fifth book he has illustrated.

He, his wife, and their two children, live in Hill Center, New Hampshire. Among his enthusiasms he lists: animals, music, and World War I airplanes.

INTO THE
WORLD'S
AMAZING
JUNGLES

JUNGLE FACTS
& FIGURES

LORI VETERE

INTO THE
WORLD'S
AMAZING
JUNGLES

Jungle Bugs & Vegetation

Jungle Facts & Figures

Jungle Tribes

Jungle Wildlife

WWF

INTO THE WORLD'S AMAZING JUNGLES

JUNGLE FACTS & FIGURES

LORI VETERE

MASON CREST

Mason Crest
450 Parkway Drive, Suite D
Broomall, Pennsylvania 19008
(866) MCP-BOOK (toll-free)
www.masoncrest.com

First printing
9 8 7 6 5 4 3 2 1

ISBN (hardback) 978-1-4222-4093-9
ISBN (series) 978-1-4222-4092-2
ISBN (ebook) 978-1-4222-7702-7

Library of Congress Cataloging-in-Publication Data

Names: Vetere, Lori, author.
Title: Jungle facts & figures / Lori Vetere.
Other titles: Jungle facts and figures
Description: Broomall, Pennsylvania : Mason Crest, [2019] | Series: Into the
  world's amazing jungles | Includes bibliographical references and index.
Identifiers: LCCN 2018013881 (print) | LCCN 2018018835 (ebook) | ISBN
  9781422277027 (eBook) | ISBN 9781422240939 (hardback) | ISBN 9781422240922
  (series)
Subjects: LCSH: Jungle ecology--Juvenile literature.
Classification: LCC QH541.5.J8 (ebook) | LCC QH541.5.J8 V48 2019 (print) |
  DDC 577.34--dc23
LC record available at https://lccn.loc.gov/2018013881

NATIONAL
HIGHLIGHTS

Developed and Produced by National Highlights Inc.
Editor: Andrew Luke
Interior and cover design: Jana Rade, impact studios
Production: Michelle Luke

CONTENTS

KEY ICONS TO LOOK FOR:

Educational Videos: Readers can view videos by scanning our QR codes, providing them with additional educational content to supplement the text. Examples include news coverage, moments in history, speeches, iconic sports moments and much more!

Series Glossary of Key Terms: This back-of-the book glossary contains terminology used throughout this series. Words found here increase the reader's ability to read and comprehend higher-level books and articles in this field.

THE CONGO

Area – 687,000 m^2 (1,780,000 km^2).

Home to: Aka tribes, Forest Leopards, Raffia Palms.

This jungle is the basin of the Congo river, covering the northern half of the Democratic Republic of the Congo and spreading west toward the Atlantic Ocean through five other countries.

More than 400 species of mammals, 700 species of fish, and 1,000 species of birds are found here.

THE AMAZON

Area – 2,123,000 m^2 (5,500,000 km^2).

Home to: Tribes of Acre, Giant Otters, Rubber trees.

About half of the world's biggest jungle is located in Brazil. The other half spreads into eight other South American countries.

The Amazon contains 20% of all the freshwater in the world.

SUNDARBANS RESERVE

Area – 4000 m^2 (10,000 km^2).

Home to: Bengal Tigers.

This region lies mostly in Bangladesh and spreads to the west into India.

The Sundarbans was declared a UNESCO World Heritage Site in 1997.

PAPUA NEW GUINEA

Area – 116,000 m^2 (300,000 km^2).

Home to: Huli tribes, Tree Kangaroos, Blue Marble trees.

The eastern half of the island of New Guinea is the country known as Papua New Guinea and was once almost completely covered by jungle. Since 1972, more than 80,000 km^2, or more than 20 percent, has been cleared.

BORNEO LOWLAND

Area – 165,000 m^2 (427,500 km2).

Home to: Penan tribes, Proboscis Monkeys, Asian Tiger Mosquitos.

This jungle encompasses the entire island of Borneo, which is shared by Brunei, Malaysia and Indonesia,

In Borneo, 700 tree species were once discovered in just 25 acres (0.1 km^2).

INTRODUCTION

The tropical jungles of this world are located close to the equator and are home to more than half of all animal and plant life found in the world today. They play a very important role in stabilizing Earth's climate by absorbing carbon dioxide and producing oxygen, which is vital for our very survival. In fact, scientists have referred to rainforests as the lungs of our planet.

Jungles should be appreciated and preserved for their role in providing a home for millions of species of plants, animals, and insects, and for their contribution of plant-derived medicines. Unfortunately, our rainforests are being destroyed at an alarming rate by loggers and builders of oil palm plantations, farms, and highways, who have prioritized the profits derived from these destructive actions over protecting our climate and the fact that they are causing many species to become either extinct or to be on the verge of extinction.

This book will focus on four of the largest tropical rainforests that exist in the world today—The Amazon Basin; the jungles of Sarawak, Borneo; the jungles of Papua New Guinea; and the vast rainforest of the Congo region in Central Africa. We will learn about the differences between tropical and temperate rainforests, the different jungle layers,

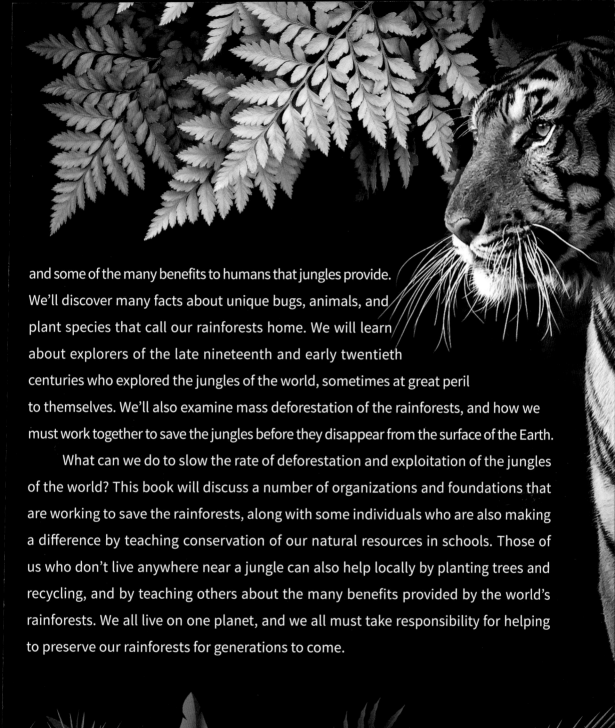

and some of the many benefits to humans that jungles provide. We'll discover many facts about unique bugs, animals, and plant species that call our rainforests home. We will learn about explorers of the late nineteenth and early twentieth centuries who explored the jungles of the world, sometimes at great peril to themselves. We'll also examine mass deforestation of the rainforests, and how we must work together to save the jungles before they disappear from the surface of the Earth.

What can we do to slow the rate of deforestation and exploitation of the jungles of the world? This book will discuss a number of organizations and foundations that are working to save the rainforests, along with some individuals who are also making a difference by teaching conservation of our natural resources in schools. Those of us who don't live anywhere near a jungle can also help locally by planting trees and recycling, and by teaching others about the many benefits provided by the world's rainforests. We all live on one planet, and we all must take responsibility for helping to preserve our rainforests for generations to come.

CHAPTER 1

Expeditions

Jungles and rainforests of the world have always been places of mystery that appeal to the adventurous spirit in all of us. What treasures are contained within? What lost cities have been hidden from the outside world, who were their inhabitants, and how did they live? Were there other secrets to be learned from finding these lost cities—perhaps a cure

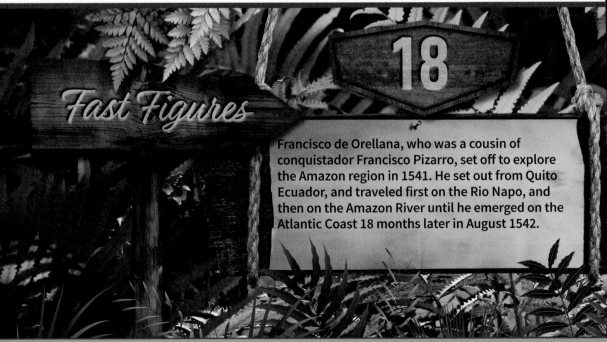

Fast Figures

18

Francisco de Orellana, who was a cousin of conquistador Francisco Pizarro, set off to explore the Amazon region in 1541. He set out from Quito Ecuador, and traveled first on the Rio Napo, and then on the Amazon River until he emerged on the Atlantic Coast 18 months later in August 1542.

British explorer Percy Fawcett returned to the Amazon seven times, ultimately disappearing into the jungle forever in his futile search for the Lost City of Z.

for cancer, or even the secret of eternal life? Here are the stories of four of these great and curious explorers.

PERCY FAWCETT AND THE LOST CITY OF Z

Percy Fawcett was a British officer, geographer, mapmaker, archaeologist, and explorer who became fascinated with tales about a lost city in the Brazilian Amazon jungle that supposedly was the remains of El Dorado (El Dorado was the legendary native city of unimaginable gold and

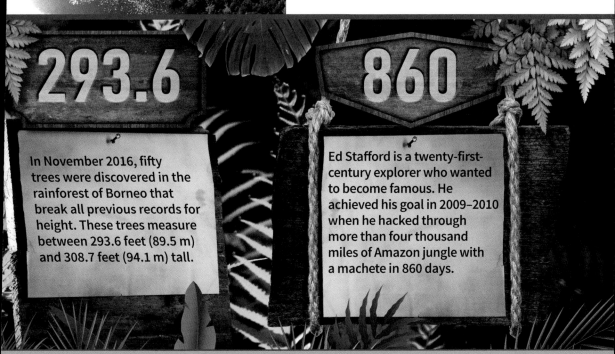

293.6

In November 2016, fifty trees were discovered in the rainforest of Borneo that break all previous records for height. These trees measure between 293.6 feet (89.5 m) and 308.7 feet (94.1 m) tall.

860

Ed Stafford is a twenty-first-century explorer who wanted to become famous. He achieved his goal in 2009–2010 when he hacked through more than four thousand miles of Amazon jungle with a machete in 860 days.

riches searched for repeatedly by the Spanish conquistadors in the sixteenth century). Fawcett first traveled to Brazil in 1907 and made seven trips in all to the Amazon jungle. Each time he returned to England with fabulous stories. Around 1914 he began to talk about a "lost" city that he called Zed (the British name for the letter Z). He became certain that ruins of this city survived and were the remnants of El Dorado and was so sure of finding it that on his last expedition in 1924 he took along his oldest son Jack (who was twenty-one at the time) and Jack's best friend. No one of the group was ever heard from again.

Dr. David Livingstone famously disappeared into the jungles of the Congo around 1865. The Scottish missionary and explorer was discovered in a town at the edge of the jungle in 1871, two years before he died of malaria.

DR. LIVINGSTONE

Dr. David Livingstone was a scientific explorer and investigator, as well as a Protestant missionary and anti-slavery campaigner, who captured the imaginations of many with his trips into "deepest, darkest Africa" to bring Christianity to African tribes. From the early 1840s to the early 1870s, Livingstone worked on mapping and navigating the rivers running through the jungle so that Europeans would be able to open up the area for converting natives to Christianity as well as to trade with them.

His exploits made him famous throughout the world. In his zeal for continued exploration, he lost contact with the world outside Africa for six years, and an explorer named Henry Morton Stanley was sent to find Livingston in March 1871. Stanley found Livingstone eight months later in a small village in Tanganyika (now known as Tanzania) and pronounced what has been one of history's most memorable greetings—"Dr. Livingstone, I presume?" Livingstone refused to leave Africa and return to "civilization." He became sick from malaria and died there in 1873.

MARY KINGSLEY

Mary Kingsley was an English explorer and writer whose travels starting in 1892 began with the hope of finishing her father's book on African culture (he had passed away the previous year). Many people, who warned her that the only non-African women to travel into dangerous territories in Africa were the wives of missionaries, frowned upon this journey. Mary ignored these prophets of doom and traveled widely in Africa, seeking out cannibals to study their religious practices, and collected previously unknown species of fish during her canoe journey on the Ogooué River. After her trip to Africa, she wrote two books and gave many lectures. She also criticized the missionaries of the Church of England for trying to convert the African people and corrupt their native religion.

LEGEND OF THE MONKEY GOD

A legend has been passed down since the 1500s about a "white city" called the City of the Monkey God, which had existed in the rainforests of Mosquitia (extending into both Nicaragua and Honduras in Central America) where explorers had located a gigantic buried statue of a monkey god. The legend said that anyone who entered this city would suddenly suffer one catastrophe after another (sickness, bad fortune, death) because it was cursed.

In 2012, an explorer named Steve Elkins decided to try to find it. Elkins had a laser mapping system with him called LIDAR, which he used to scan the dense jungle by positioning it over a hole cut in the bottom of a Cessna airplane. He located what appeared to be the remains of an ancient city and got the support of National Geographic to return by land and locate the site. These modern-day explorers found carved stones and other artifacts dating to the sixteenth century.

After the explorers returned home they began to suffer from a disease called Leishmaniasis, which is caused by a sand fly bite and causes parasites to start eating away your lips and nose until, if not medically treated, they actually fall off your face. Is this, indeed, the curse of the monkey god?

Learn about the modern-day search for the Ancient Lost City of the Monkey God in Honduras.

Locations

AMAZON RAINFOREST

The Amazon rainforest is so big that there are portions of it in nine different countries—Brazil, Colombia, Peru, Bolivia, Ecuador, Guyana, Venezuela, French Guiana, and Suriname. Brazil has the largest percentage of this massive jungle—around 60%, followed by Bolivia, Peru, and Ecuador. Besides its ranking as the largest jungle on Earth, the Amazon is home to one of the world's largest river systems. This enormous and beautiful land covers about 2.1 million square miles.

Many tourists enter Brazil's Amazon region by catching a boat ride in the city of Manaus that will cruise up and down the beautiful Amazon River. There are amazing places to check out, like the Jaú National Park, the Lago Janauri Ecological Park, and the Anavilhanas Archipelago. A favorite of visitors is a trip to see the Meeting of the Waters, where the sand-colored water of the Rio Solimões (Solimões River) meets the dark black waters of the Rio Negro (Black River).

The Brazilian city of Manaus lies near the headwaters of the Amazon, the heart of the world's largest river system.

Fast Figures

16,502

New Guinea, which lies about four degrees south of the Equator, is Earth's only tropical island to possess a glacier (glaciers are usually only found in locations much farther north or south that have much higher altitudes). This glacier is named Puncak Jaya, and at 16,502 feet (5,030 m) is the tallest point in the entire Pacific southwest.

BORNEO RAINFORESTS

The Borneo lowland rainforests are divided up into several areas on the great island of Borneo located in Southeast Asia. They cover an area of approximately 165,100 square miles over four different political territories—Sarawak and Sabah, owned by Malaysia; Kalimantan, which is part of Indonesia; and Brunei. The Borneo rainforests were known for many years as the richest jungles on Earth and boasted about ten thousand plant species (that's more than can be found on the entire African continent), more than two thousand species of orchids and three thousand species of trees, of which 155 are found only on Borneo. Due to the immense threats of logging and conversion of the rainforest to giant industrial oil palm and rubber plantations, this entire region of rainforest shrinking rapidly.

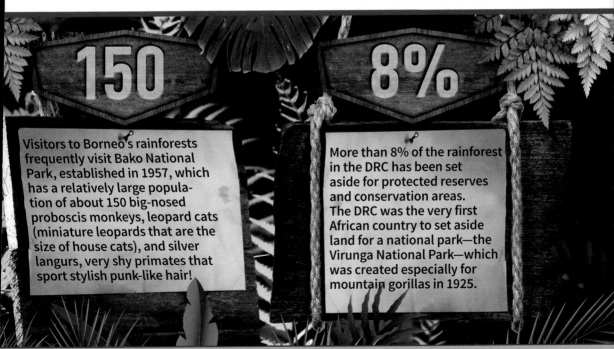

150

Visitors to Borneo's rainforests frequently visit Bako National Park, established in 1957, which has a relatively large population of about 150 big-nosed proboscis monkeys, leopard cats (miniature leopards that are the size of house cats), and silver langurs, very shy primates that sport stylish punk-like hair!

8%

More than 8% of the rainforest in the DRC has been set aside for protected reserves and conservation areas. The DRC was the very first African country to set aside land for a national park—the Virunga National Park—which was created especially for mountain gorillas in 1925.

PAPUA NEW GUINEA RAINFORESTS

The jungles on the island of New Guinea are located in the Eastern province of Papua and are the third-largest mass of tropical forests on Earth, only surpassed by the Amazon region and the Congo Basin. Rainforests cover 65% of the island of New Guinea—178,954 miles (288,000 km)—and contain both lowland and mountainous areas. More than

Gorillas roam the jungles of the Congo Basin, which spans five countries in central Africa.

twenty-five thousand different species of plants and 760 unique bird species call these rainforests their home. Unfortunately, industrial mining and logging and the conversion of these beautiful forests into flat, treeless farmland all threaten these beautiful lands.

CONGO RAINFOREST

The Congo Rainforest covers a large area of Central and Western Equatorial Africa and is located in the Democratic Republic of Congo (DRC), Cameroon, Gabon, Equatorial Guinea, and the Central African Republic. It is the second-largest jungle in the world with 1.4 million square miles (3.7 million sq km)—only the Amazon rainforest is larger—and it contains about 18% of Earth's remaining tropical jungle. The DRC possesses two-thirds of this enormous rainforest. The Congo River, the second-largest river on Earth, flows through this jungle into the Atlantic Ocean.

The Amazon Rainforest Facts – This video contains some amazing facts about the jungles of the Amazon Basin.

CHAPTER 3

Conservation Stories

Tropical rainforests are vanishing from the face of the Earth. The good news is that their loss can be stopped, slowed down, or even reversed in some cases. Concerned people around the world are working on conservation efforts that still allow some sustainable use of the rainforest, while at the same time restoring

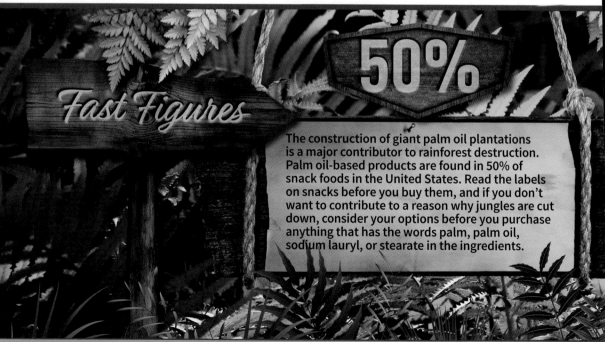

Fast Figures

50%

The construction of giant palm oil plantations is a major contributor to rainforest destruction. Palm oil-based products are found in 50% of snack foods in the United States. Read the labels on snacks before you buy them, and if you don't want to contribute to a reason why jungles are cut down, consider your options before you purchase anything that has the words palm, palm oil, sodium lauryl, or stearate in the ingredients.

and rehabilitating areas that have been degraded and also establishing new protected areas.

Experts throughout the world agree that if the jungles are left intact and are instead harvested for their many fruits, nuts, medicinal plants and oil-producing plants, they would provide more economic value than simply cutting down the forest for its timber or to create cattle ranches.

The following conservation stories will highlight individuals who have spoken out about how the jungle is important to the environment and how we can restore many damaged rainforests by replanting trees in the same locations where they've been cut down. They also encourage local people to change their lifestyles so that what they do doesn't harm the environment, work to establish parks and reserves to protect wildlife and plant life, and support those companies that strive to minimize the level of environmental damage they cause.

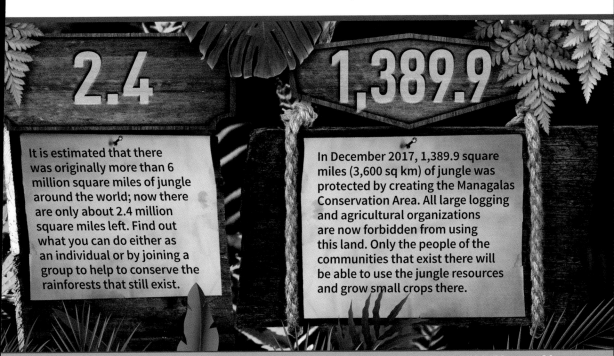

2.4

It is estimated that there was originally more than 6 million square miles of jungle around the world; now there are only about 2.4 million square miles left. Find out what you can do either as an individual or by joining a group to help to conserve the rainforests that still exist.

1,389.9

In December 2017, 1,389.9 square miles (3,600 sq km) of jungle was protected by creating the Managalas Conservation Area. All large logging and agricultural organizations are now forbidden from using this land. Only the people of the communities that exist there will be able to use the jungle resources and grow small crops there.

The clearing of jungles to allow for huge palm oil plantations is a major conservation issue.

AMAZON REGION

Diana Rios is a member of the Ashéninka tribe of Saweto, Peru. Her father, Edwin Chota, was active for more than ten years in the fight to obtain a legal title for the tribe's ancestral lands and to protect the jungle from illegal loggers. In September 2014 Chota, along with three other leaders of the Ashéninka tribe, was brutally murdered by illegal loggers. Fortunately, the outside world found out about this terrible event and members of the Rainforest Foundation US have been working tirelessly on the tribe's behalf. On August 19, 2015, the Peruvian government gave the tribe the land title for two hundred thousand acres of rainforest, all the land around their town of Saweto.

BORNEO

Jackson Helms and his wife Sara were students at the University of Oklahoma when they began to hear stories about the devastation of the rainforest in Borneo. They decided to move to Borneo and formed the organization Health in Harmony, with the goal of saving jungles and saving lives. They monitor the land encircling Gunung Palung National Park for signs of deforestation, illegal farm clearings, sawmills, and logging roads. They check satellite images to keep track of what is happening deep within the jungle. They provide training and assistance to people who decide to pursue more jungle-friendly careers. They even run a chainsaw buyback program to get chainsaws out of the jungle.

Diana Rios: Rainforest Defender – Diana Rios is a member of the Ashéninka tribe of Saweto, Peru. After her father and other community leaders were murdered, Diana took over their role as defender of the rainforest.

CONGO BASIN RAINFOREST

Rainforest Foundation UK works to protect the jungles of the Congo Basin.

Simon Counsell, the executive director of Rainforest Foundation UK, spoke out in 2016 about how heavy-handed efforts to protect the region's rainforests are making matters worse. Some organizations have spent money on "eco-guards" (armed guards who patrol the borders of the rainforest to protect the wildlife), a step that backfired when some of these guards ended up hurting local people by evicting them from their homes and even burning them down. Mr. Counsell called for organizations to instead contribute to creating a few "community forests" where local tribes people can practice their centuries-old customs of hunting and gathering only what they can use.

CHAPTER 4

Climate

Jungles around the world have several things in common—their climate is extremely humid because it rains at least ninety days a year (which creates a total of 8.2 feet (250 cm) of rainfall a year)—and in between the rainy days, the sun shines brightly. The closer the rainforest is to the equator, the hotter it will be. This combination of factors means that an extremely large number of plants and trees will thrive. It also means that the topmost canopy of the jungle is crowded with leafy branches, which in turn crowd out the understory plants from getting much sunlight. To fight this condition, the plants on the forest floor have learned to survive by growing as vines on taller plants and even growing on the branches of taller trees so that they will get sunlight.

Sadly, the natural order of life in the jungles of our planet is being dramatically affected by climate change.

PAPUA NEW GUINEA RAINFOREST

The rainforest of Papua New Guinea is tropical—the coastal plains average 82.4 °F (28° C) and the mountain and inland regions average 78.8° F (26° C). The humidity of this area is high, usually between 70% and 90%. There is a dry season between June to

September and a rainy season from December to March. This area experiences monsoons (wind direction shifts that cause dry spells in winter and heavy rainfall in summer) and typhoons (giant storms which can cause extreme damage, soil erosion, and flooding).

BORNEO RAINFORESTS

The rainforests of Sarawak, Borneo, are estimated to be 130 million years old, older even than the Amazonian rainforest. These lowland jungles, with a very stable average temperature ranging between 77° F (25° C) and 91.5° F (33° C) are situated in a tropical monsoon zone. This means that they experience severe rainstorms for certain times of the year. The stable climate of this area has created an amazing environment for about ten thousand plant species to grow (more than exist on the entire African continent).

Unfortunately, along with the destruction of more than 80% of its rainforests, Borneo has begun to be affected by severe climate change and now has a greatly

Fast Figures

64.4

A region is said to have a monsoon climate when its driest month averages less than 2.4 inches (60 mm) of precipitation, but accounts for more than 4% of all the region's precipitation for the year. This is the case with many of the jungle regions in South and Central America. There is no month when the temperature drops below an average of 64.4 °F (18 °C).

increased risk of both forest fires and flooding. There are actions that people are taking to help Borneo survive climate change. Volunteers are going into the jungle and counting the number of tree seedlings that are present and how close together they are growing. They are planting new seedlings and assisting in measuring the survival and growth of the seedlings. Scientists are measuring the amount of carbon in plants and evaluating how much carbon is being stored and how much is decomposing.

Tropical jungles get at least ninety rainy days per year.

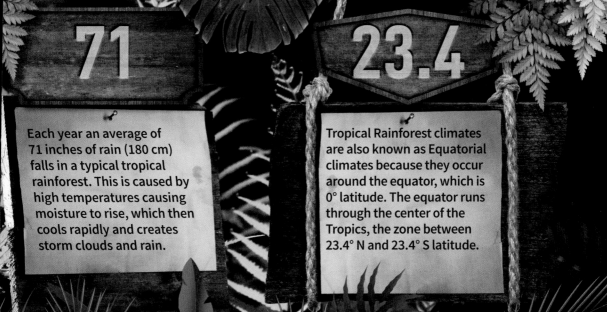

71

Each year an average of 71 inches of rain (180 cm) falls in a typical tropical rainforest. This is caused by high temperatures causing moisture to rise, which then cools rapidly and creates storm clouds and rain.

23.4

Tropical Rainforest climates are also known as Equatorial climates because they occur around the equator, which is 0° latitude. The equator runs through the center of the Tropics, the zone between 23.4° N and 23.4° S latitude.

Others are sorting and collecting specimens of insects, plants, and other animals, measuring the amount of rainfall, counting the different types of vegetation and observing how much canopy cover there is. Finally, volunteers are measuring the amount of soil erosion that is present and analyzing and collecting many different soil samples.

CONGO RAINFOREST

The Central African Congo rainforest lies primarily in the Democratic Republic of Congo. This area enjoys an average temperature of 77° F (25° C) and

The wet climate in the Congo means thick vegetation in the jungles. The dense canopy blocks much of the sun, so ground vegetation sends lianas, which are thick vines, up the trees in search of sunlight.

has an average rainfall of 58 inches (147 cm) each year. This climate has allowed dense vegetation to grow, and in some parts of the jungle, only about 1% of sunlight is able to reach the ground. For this reason, ground vegetation has developed over thousands of years into thick vines called lianas which are able to grow as long as 3,000 feet (914 m) to reach some sunlight.

Researchers have reported that climate change is causing drastic changes in the rainforest. For one thing, the jungle is becoming a lot less green. This is caused by a lower amount of total rainfall and a lesser amount of water storage underneath the canopy. The tropical jungle appears to be under great stress due to water shortages and the drier, warmer climate of the twenty-first century.

AMAZON RIVER REGION RAINFOREST

The Amazon rainforest averages temperatures of about 82.4 °F (28° C) all year long and is very humid. Because of the tropical heat and its large river basin, moist air nearest the ground is heated up, making it rise until it reaches a condensation point and forms rain clouds. This causes frequent monsoon-like conditions.

Because of extensive deforestation, the rainfall totals of the Amazon rainforest are decreasing. In fact, this area suffered its worst drought in more than one hundred years in 2005.

Journalist Justin Catanoso on Climate Change in the Rainforest – Justin Catanoso is an expert on climate change and has won a Pulitzer Prize for his coverage of the topic.

CHAPTER 5

Plant-Derived Medicines

Since prehistoric days, our ancestors who lived in the jungles of the world have studied the plants around them. The men and women who were the most knowledgeable

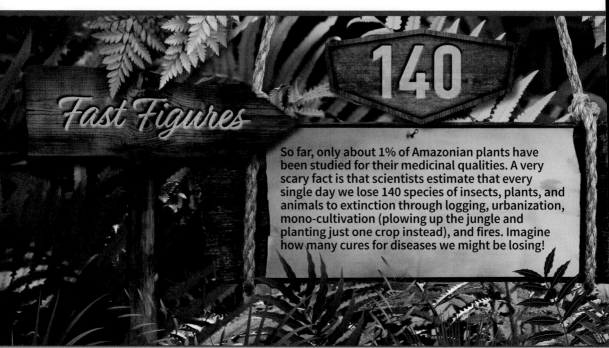

Fast Figures

140

So far, only about 1% of Amazonian plants have been studied for their medicinal qualities. A very scary fact is that scientists estimate that every single day we lose 140 species of insects, plants, and animals to extinction through logging, urbanization, mono-cultivation (plowing up the jungle and planting just one crop instead), and fires. Imagine how many cures for diseases we might be losing!

about these plants became the shamans (medicine men and women) of the tribes, and it was to these shamans that the tribes people came when they were suffering from both physical and spiritual ailments. The jungle medicines of the Amazon River region, Borneo, the Congo rainforest, and the jungles of Papua New Guinea are being studied today for possible use in modern medicines.

Papua New Guinea

GOAT WEED (AGERATUM CONYZOIDES)

This annual herb is noted for its very strong disgusting odor and its purple or green hairy stem (it really makes you wonder why on Earth anyone would want to eat this plant in the first place)! The leaves are crushed and mixed with water and then given to a patient

6%

Did you know that rainforests cover only 6% of the world's surface, but they are home to more than 50% of the plant species growing on Earth today?

25%

25% of our Western medicines have their origin in rainforest plants and trees.

Goat weed is used to treat intestinal ailments like diarrhea and dysentery.

that has either diarrhea or dysentery to drink, and the crushed leaves themselves are rubbed vigorously on a patient's forehead to make headaches go away. The juice of the crushed leaves is applied to cuts, bruises, sores, and wounds.

GORAGORA (ALPINIA OCEANICA BURKILL)

This perennial herb is found in the moist jungles of Papua New Guinea. Its fresh leaves are either chewed by children and adults alike for a sore tongue or used for covering up wounds.

Amazon Jungle

Shamans have known about and used many Amazon rainforest plants that have medicinal qualities. Some of these plants have been used to make quinine (which treats malaria and severe leg cramps), muscle relaxants, blood thinners, antibiotics, cancer drugs, and anti-parasitic drugs (which cure roundworm infections and hookworm).

AMAZONIAN SODO PLANT

This odorous plant is being used instead of nicotine patches to cure tobacco addiction and also an addiction to alcohol.

Congo Rainforest

A study is being done of traditional medicinal plants found in the Congo that are useful for treating malaria. To date, Western researchers have found 120 jungle plants that that seem highly likely to be useful against this terrible disease, which is the number one cause of death in the Democratic Republic of Congo. Many studies have been done on rats, but it is hoped that studies can now be done using humans.

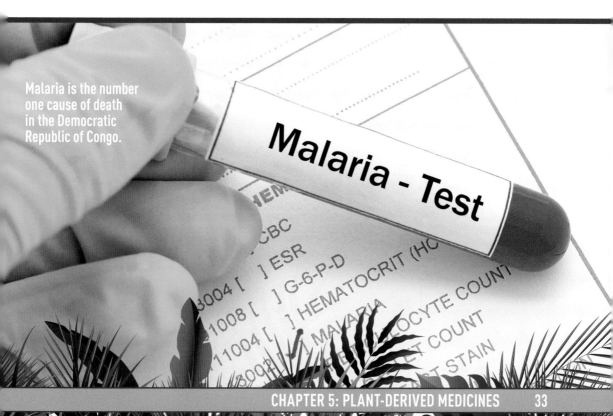

Malaria is the number one cause of death in the Democratic Republic of Congo.

Borneo Rainforest

The jungles of Borneo contain upwards of fifteen thousand species of plants, many of which have been used for medicinal purposes by the local tribespeople. For example, there is a shrub in Sarawak known as Kelabuno that contains a substance called silvestrol, which has been shown to be just as effective as chemotherapy in destroying different types of cancer cells, especially nose cancer cells.

Compounds have been discovered in tree latex that have the possibility of curing many different types of HIV, and substances found inside the langsat tree's bark have been found to have antimalarial qualities. Who knows what other types of cures might be found in Sarawak, where more than eight thousand plant species and two thousand tree species are found?

Medicinal Plants Of The Amazon Rainforest – This fascinating video shows Kendalyn Hersh, a Radford University student, teach a group of visitors about the value of Amazonian medicinal plants.

Types of Jungles

Tropical Rainforests

Tropical rainforests grow in parts of the world that are located close to the equator (an imaginary line that is drawn around our Earth at an equal distance from both the North Pole and the South Pole that has a latitude of 0°). These are areas that do not experience a dry season. The World Wildlife Fund classifies them as moist tropical broadleaf forests.

Tropical rainforests are hot, wet forests that have different layers of vegetation—the forest floor, understory, canopy, and emergent layers. The upper layers are so filled with tree branches and plants that only the smallest amount of light is able to reach the ground. This means that there are few plants on the ground level, and that makes it easy to walk through.

Tropical rainforests are in zones of the world close to the equator that have hot, wet climates.

100

Fast Figures

The brown-throated three-toed sloth lives totally in tropical rainforest trees; eats fruit, leaves, and twigs; and moves so incredibly slowly that algae grows on its fur and colors it a green shade. The capybara, the biggest rodent on Earth, weighs over 100 pounds, stands about 2 feet tall, and can hold its breath underwater for up to five minutes when it is hiding from predators.

ARE JUNGLES DIFFERENT FROM RAINFORESTS?

The terms jungle and tropical rainforest are interchangeable in common usage. The scientific community began referring to jungles as tropical rainforests about forty years ago. The people who study them do make a distinction between the two. Jungles is reserved for reference to sections of rainforests that have so much vegetation growing in them that it is almost impossible to walk through without a machete or other cutting tool. Jungles require a lot of unrestricted sunlight as well as plentiful rainfall for a good portion of the year. They can be found growing along the edges of the rainforest or alongside rivers inside the rainforest, as well as in locations where rainforest trees have been either knocked down by a natural disaster (hurricanes or any type of high wind) or cut down by humans, leaving land uncovered. Despite this narrow distinction, people have been using the words jungle and rainforest to mean the same thing since the 1970s.

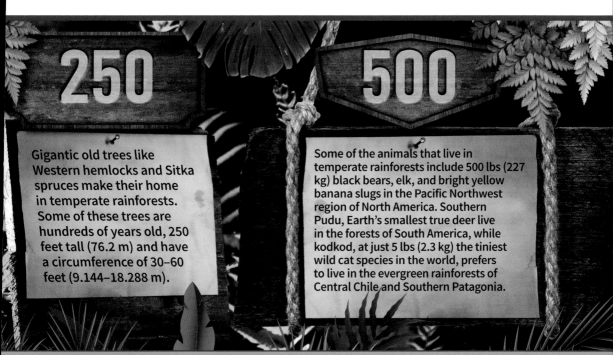

Gigantic old trees like Western hemlocks and Sitka spruces make their home in temperate rainforests. Some of these trees are hundreds of years old, 250 feet tall (76.2 m) and have a circumference of 30–60 feet (9.144–18.288 m).

Some of the animals that live in temperate rainforests include 500 lbs (227 kg) black bears, elk, and bright yellow banana slugs in the Pacific Northwest region of North America. Southern Pudu, Earth's smallest true deer live in the forests of South America, while kodkod, at just 5 lbs (2.3 kg) the tiniest wild cat species in the world, prefers to live in the evergreen rainforests of Central Chile and Southern Patagonia.

TEMPERATE RAINFORESTS

Temperate rainforests have a very rainy (or sometimes even snowy) climate and exist in northern latitudes along the coastline, with most temperate rainforests situated on the northwest coast of North America from southern Alaska down to northern California. They can also be found in small areas of New Zealand, southern Chile, and Australia. The climate is cool in these rainforests, with an annual average temperature of about 68° F (20° C).

Unlike tropical jungles, temperate rainforests have far fewer species of trees (like this Western red cedar), many of which can live for more than a century.

SIMILARITIES BETWEEN TROPICAL AND TEMPERATE RAINFORESTS

Both temperate and tropical rainforests have tall, dense, and very green vegetation, and most of the trees found in both forests flare at the base. They are both rich in animal and plant species, although there is more diversity present in tropical rainforests. Both forests enjoy a very wet climate. While tropical rainforests get between 80–100 inches (203.2–254 cm) of rainfall each year, temperate rainforests get around 100 inches (254 cm) annually.

DIFFERENCES BETWEEN TEMPERATE AND TROPICAL RAINFORESTS

Temperate rainforests are cool, while tropical rainforests are hot. A tropical rainforest has many hundreds of different broadleaf tree species that live to be between 50–100 years old. In contrast, temperate rainforests have only a few (10–20) types of tree species, often have needles instead of leaves, and can live to be between 500–1,000 years old! Both rainforests have epiphytes (plants that grow on other plants but receive their nutrients from either the air or the rain). Temperate epiphytes are usually ferns and mosses, while tropical epiphytes have a large variety of plants including bromeliads and orchids.

Temperate And Tropical Forest Ecosystems – This lighthearted video clearly explains some facts about both tropical and temperate rainforest ecosystems.

CHAPTER 7

Verge of Extinction?

The natural rate of extinction on our planet is approximately one species each year. Because of deforestation, species are becoming extinct 3–4 times more rapidly. Scientists estimate that each day we lose 136 animal, plant, and insect species—more than fifty thousand species a year. How many of those lost species might have provided a cure

Fast Figures

5,000

Many species of mammals are critically endangered in the Congo rainforest. The list of endangered mammals includes the African slender-snouted crocodile, the Pohle's fruit bat, and the Pennant's red colobus monkey, of which there are fewer than 5,000 left.

for a life-threatening disease?

Half of all animals on planet Earth live in the rainforests. They can only survive if they have a sufficient source of water, food, and shelter, and if there is a balance between prey (the hunted) and predator (the hunter). These animals will become endangered if the ecosystem around them is destroyed, perhaps due to an excessive amount of polluted soil, water, or air; or if the area they live in is overhunted, overfished, or overdeveloped, among many other reasons. We must do all that we can to save both plants and animals that are on the verge of extinction so that our children and future generations can enjoy and learn from them.

Orchid species, like this *Sobralia Rosea* seen in the Ecuadorian Amazon, are all facing extinction in the Amazon jungle.

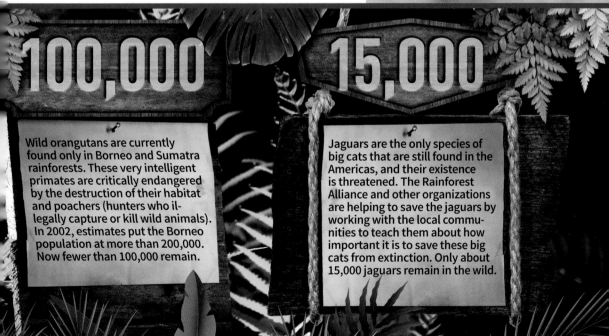

100,000

Wild orangutans are currently found only in Borneo and Sumatra rainforests. These very intelligent primates are critically endangered by the destruction of their habitat and poachers (hunters who illegally capture or kill wild animals). In 2002, estimates put the Borneo population at more than 200,000. Now fewer than 100,000 remain.

15,000

Jaguars are the only species of big cats that are still found in the Americas, and their existence is threatened. The Rainforest Alliance and other organizations are helping to save the jaguars by working with the local communities to teach them about how important it is to save these big cats from extinction. Only about 15,000 jaguars remain in the wild.

Endangered Animal Species of the Jungle

AMAZON

Giant Otters

Giant otters, one of the most famous animals that live in the Amazon jungle, are now on the endangered list. Their existence is threatened because of the destruction of their habitat by deforestation, an increased human population, and also the increased number of hunters that are killing them for their pelts.

Habitat destruction from deforestation has landed the giant otter of the Amazon on the endangered species list.

Poison Dart Frogs

The Amazon rainforest is home to 234 different species of poison dart frogs. These beautiful but deadly frogs come in many different colors and are only 1–2 inches long (2.54–5.08 cm). The poison which is released from their skin has been used for centuries by Amazonian natives to poison blowgun dart tips. Just because humans have taken advantage of their self-preservation trait doesn't mean that they should become extinct because their rainforest habitat is ruined!

THE CONGO

There are nine land species and a number of marine species that are endangered in the Congo rainforest because of deforestation, habitat destruction, illegal exotic pet traders, and hunting. Some of these endangered animals are the bonobo, the Eastern gorilla, the African wild dog, the Egyptian vulture, and three species of amphibians. Twenty-one freshwater fish species are endangered because of habitat erosion, pollution, agricultural chemicals, and illegal unregulated fishing.

Endangered Plant Species of the Rainforests
AMAZON RAINFOREST

Many of the rainforest plants in the Amazon are either endangered or on the verge of extinction because of deforestation, intensive logging and farming, commercial development, and orchid hunters. Because of the global craze for orchids, practically all of the twenty-five thousand orchid species are threatened or endangered, and some of them are already extinct.

PAPUA NEW GUINEA RAINFOREST

Tropical hardwood trees from the rainforests of New Guinea are highly threatened by intensive logging and exportation. Especially vulnerable are those trees that produce agarwood, a very fragrant heartwood formed in the roots and trunks of incense trees. A fungus has infected many of these trees and overharvesting will soon leave no healthy trees in existence.

SARAWAK BORNEO RAINFOREST

The giant rafflesia flower (the largest and heaviest flower on Earth) is becoming an endangered species in the jungles of Sarawak in Borneo due to deforestation, pollution, and increased human activity and urbanization. This famous flower (which smells like rotting flesh and only blooms once a year for 3–5 days) is a parasitic plant and has to rely on tetrastigma vines to grow and prosper, which are also becoming rare. This plant's existence is also threatened because people have harvested it too frequently to use it for medicinal purposes.

Endangered Species In The Amazon – A well done school project concerning endangered Amazon region species.

CHAPTER 8

Human Uses: Products That Come from the Jungle

Rainforests are the gardens of Earth. There are literally thousands of foods, medicines, oils, extracts, and wood that either have their origin in the jungle or are still being produced there today. Unfortunately, as the rainforests keep shrinking because of monoculture (the growth or cultivation of one single crop on land that was previously jungle) the number and type of different products available keep being reduced. The worst offenders in this type of agriculture are palm oil plantations and rubber tree plantations.

AMAZON RIVER REGION

Dr. Drauzio Varella is a Brazilian cancer specialist who began to explore the Amazon rainforest in 1995 for plant extracts from trees and plants that could serve as natural medicines useful for treating various types of cancer. He and his team have collected more than two thousand extracts to date. Of these extracts, more than seventy have been found to have an impact on tumor cells, and fifty have been demonstrated to be effective against bacterial infections.

SARAWAK, BORNEO

The lowland rainforest in Borneo at one time had 267 different species of hardwood trees, of which 60% were not found anywhere else in the world. Many of these trees are esteemed because

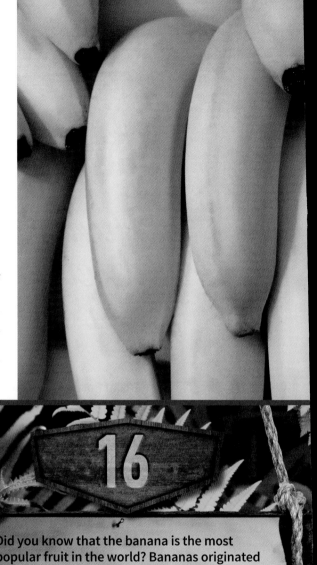

Fast Figures

16

Did you know that the banana is the most popular fruit in the world? Bananas originated in the rainforests of Central America and were first imported to the United States in 1870; by 1898, Americans were eating more than 16 million bunches each year!

The banana is the world's most popular fruit. Americans alone eat millions of bunches every year.

the furniture made from them lasts for hundreds of years, and the resins and oils that they contain are also valuable. Once these trees were cut down, giant oil palm plantations were built in the jungle. Palm oil is used throughout the world for cooking oil as a substitute for butter and to make biodiesel fuel.

CONGO RIVER REGION

Valuable trees in the Congo Basin forest are being illegally cut and sent around the world to use for both furniture and

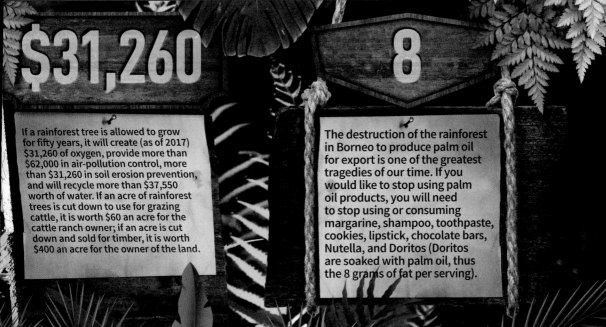

$31,260

If a rainforest tree is allowed to grow for fifty years, it will create (as of 2017) $31,260 of oxygen, provide more than $62,000 in air-pollution control, more than $31,260 in soil erosion prevention, and will recycle more than $37,550 worth of water. If an acre of rainforest trees is cut down to use for grazing cattle, it is worth $60 an acre for the cattle ranch owner; if an acre is cut down and sold for timber, it is worth $400 an acre for the owner of the land.

8

The destruction of the rainforest in Borneo to produce palm oil for export is one of the greatest tragedies of our time. If you would like to stop using palm oil products, you will need to stop using or consuming margarine, shampoo, toothpaste, cookies, lipstick, chocolate bars, Nutella, and Doritos (Doritos are soaked with palm oil, thus the 8 grams of fat per serving).

flooring. The local markets in the DRC are an important way for rainforest products to be sold and traded. One of the most popular products are kola (also spelled cola) nuts, which contain caffeine and are used to make products around the world (Coca-Cola, Pepsi Cola, etc.). Other products derived from the Congo rainforest are palm wine, charcoal, rattans (palm tree stems that are used to make furniture and are similar to wicker products), all kinds of spices, and dried fruits and vegetables.

More than seventy years of logging has severely depleted the jungles of Papua New Guinea.

WARNING
FOREST HARVESTING

PAPUA NEW GUINEA

The timber available for export from the Papua New Guinea rainforests is scarce since they have been logged and exploited for more than seventy years. Taun wood is still illegally exported to China, which processes the wood and then sells it to the United States via large companies like Home Depot. Rainforest products that are valued in the world economy include oil and other mineral fuels, waxes, vegetable and animal fats, fish, coffee, and spices. Other jungle products include copper ore, gold, nickel, sugar, rubber, cocoa, and tea.

What Products Come From Rainforests? – A good introductory video demonstrating some of the many products that come from rainforests.

Species Figures

AMAZON RAINFOREST

The Amazon tropical rainforest is one of the most bio-diverse (having a very large variety of animal and plant species) regions in the world. It has 433 species of mammals, 237 species of reptiles, 222 amphibian species, 1,300 bird species, over eighteen thousand different plant varieties, and more primates and freshwater fish exist there than in any other area on Earth. Just one acre of the Amazon jungle is estimated to contain 750 different types of trees and nine hundred tons of live plants.

Visitors to the Amazon tropical rainforest may see black caiman (large carnivorous reptiles that are the largest predators in the Amazon region), cougars, wild piranhas, anaconda snakes, gigantic hairy spiders, and even a vampire bat or two. The only way to travel safely through this entire region is by boat, accompanied by trained guides.

PAPUA NEW GUINEA RAINFORESTS

The rainforests of Papua New Guinea, located immediately south of the equator and about one hundred miles to the north of Australia, are also best explored with well-

The black caiman is just one of the 237 reptile species found in the Amazon jungle.

trained tour guides. Guides can accompany you through beautiful mountain ranges covered with jungles, amazing limestone canyons, and an endless array of swampland. These rainforests contain seven hundred different bird species (including birds of paradise, parrots, and kingfishers), more than 250 mammal species, and more than nine thousand plant species. There are even sixty different species of marsupials, including the incredible tree kangaroos and the Papuan forest wallabies. Cassowaries, a colorful relative of the emu, are common here. In fact, they can only be found in the jungles of New Guinea and in parts of northern Australia.

The red-bellied sculptor squirrel of Borneo is the smallest squirrel in the world.

CONGO RAINFOREST

The Congo rainforest contains about 70% of all the plant cover in Africa. It has six hundred different tree species, two hundred amphibian species, 450 mammal species, three hundred reptile species, one thousand bird species and almost ten thousand plant species, of which 3,300 are

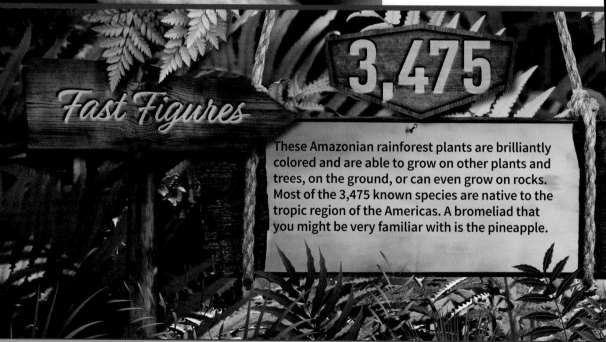

Fast Figures

3,475

These Amazonian rainforest plants are brilliantly colored and are able to grow on other plants and trees, on the ground, or can even grow on rocks. Most of the 3,475 known species are native to the tropic region of the Americas. A bromeliad that you might be very familiar with is the pineapple.

only found in this region of the world. The Congo basin is unique because it's the only place on Earth where three subspecies of gorillas are found—the lowland, Eastern lowland, and giant mountain gorilla. Other interesting animals of the Congo jungle are the hippopotamus, which lives by the Congo River, the smaller African forest elephant (which has tusks that project downward), the okapi, and Allen's swamp monkey.

SARAWAK BORNEO RAINFOREST

There are 288 land mammal species and ninety-one species of marine mammals found in and around the rainforests of Borneo. Its mammal list contains sixty-one different species of mice and rats and 102 different bat species. Some of the most interesting mammals found in this list include the world's smallest squirrel, the red-bellied sculptor squirrel, the pouched tomb bat, the hollow-faced bat, Bornean bearded pigs, the clouded leopard, the hairy-nosed otter, and the Bornean white-bearded gibbon.

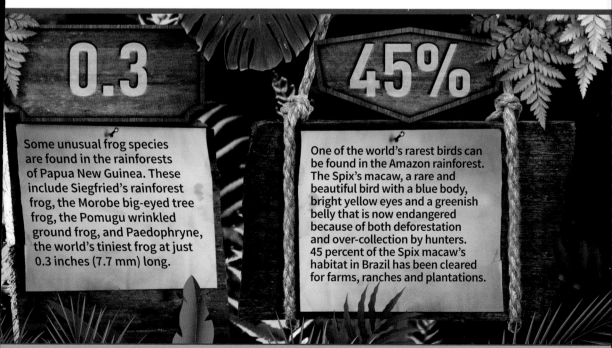

0.3

Some unusual frog species are found in the rainforests of Papua New Guinea. These include Siegfried's rainforest frog, the Morobe big-eyed tree frog, the Pomugu wrinkled ground frog, and Paedophryne, the world's tiniest frog at just 0.3 inches (7.7 mm) long.

45%

One of the world's rarest birds can be found in the Amazon rainforest. The Spix's macaw, a rare and beautiful bird with a blue body, bright yellow eyes and a greenish belly that is now endangered because of both deforestation and over-collection by hunters. 45 percent of the Spix macaw's habitat in Brazil has been cleared for farms, ranches and plantations.

In the plant world, Borneo has three thousand different tree species, one thousand different ferns, and two thousand species of orchids. In just 3.86 square miles (10 sq km) there are more types of plants and trees than all of Europe and North America combined. Borneo's ironwood tree (called Belian) is the hardest and heaviest of all of the jungle trees. It grows extremely slowly and is so heavy that termites aren't able to bite through it. It also sinks rather than floats on water. Unfortunately, loggers have cut down millions of these noble trees and now only a few remain in the remotest sections of the rainforest.

Exploring Ecosystems: Tropical Rainforest Diversity (California Academy Of Sciences) – This is a good introductory video about the diversity of tropical rainforests created by the California Academy of Sciences.

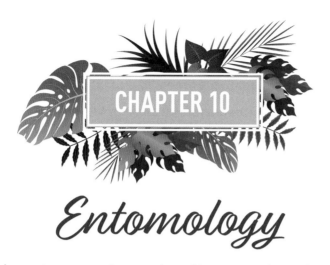

CHAPTER 10

Entomology

Rainforests are home to an amazing number of insect species. Scientists estimate that there are possibly ten million different insect species in the world, and a great number of these species live in the tropical jungles. In a recent survey conducted in a Panamanian rainforest (the San Lorenzo Forest), it was discovered that one acre of rainforest was

Just a single acre of this jungle in Panama can contain more than six thousand species of insects.

home to six thousand species of insects, and that the entire jungle contained 25,246 arthropods (spider, insect, and crustacean) species!

The rainforests of the Amazon, Borneo, Papua New Guinea, and the Congo are also teeming with insects. Let's take a look at some of the most interesting and unique bugs that have chosen to make these jungles their home sweet home.

Congo

AFRICAN WEAVER ANTS OF THE CONGO

African weaver ants act like living glue guns that create their nests out of hollowed balls of leaves. The larvae that they discharge are silken and glue-filled. Working together, some ants make living chains in the treetops while other ants move the

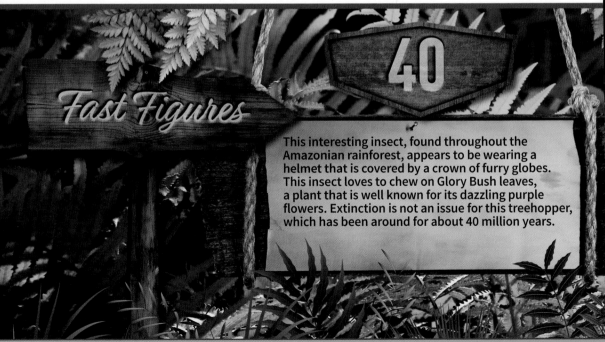

Fast Figures

40

This interesting insect, found throughout the Amazonian rainforest, appears to be wearing a helmet that is covered by a crown of furry globes. This insect loves to chew on Glory Bush leaves, a plant that is well known for its dazzling purple flowers. Extinction is not an issue for this treehopper, which has been around for about 40 million years.

larvae back and forth along the chain, gluing the edges of the leaves together at the same time. These very aggressive ants can then roam the treetops for prey that they use to feed to the larvae.

Amazon Jungle

SULFUR AND HELICONIUS BUTTERFLIES

About one hundred years ago Henry Bates, an explorer of the Amazon rainforest, noted a very strange behavior among some orange or yellow butterflies. They gathered around the eyes of turtles and drank their eye fluids to get sodium and other necessary minerals. The butterflies often fed on poisonous plants and absorbed the toxins of these plants into their tissues, which gave them protection by making them bad to eat!

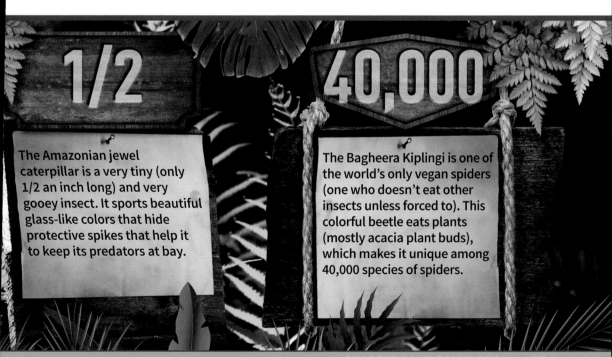

1/2

The Amazonian jewel caterpillar is a very tiny (only 1/2 an inch long) and very gooey insect. It sports beautiful glass-like colors that hide protective spikes that help it to keep its predators at bay.

40,000

The Bagheera Kiplingi is one of the world's only vegan spiders (one who doesn't eat other insects unless forced to). This colorful beetle eats plants (mostly acacia plant buds), which makes it unique among 40,000 species of spiders.

Papua New Guinea Rainforest
THE GIANT BURROWING COCKROACH

The giant burrowing cockroach of the New Guinea rainforest is also known as the litter bug and the rhinoceros cockroach. The Earth's heaviest cockroach can weigh 1.2 ounces, can measure 3.1 inches in length, and can live up to ten years! They make their homes by burrowing down about three feet into the soil. These giant insects do their part for the ecosystem by eating dead leaves, especially eucalyptus leaves.

The male stalk-eyed fly attracts females based on the length of its eye stalks.

Sarawak Borneo Rainforest
THE STALK-EYED FLY AND THE WHIP SCORPION

Studies in the jungles of Borneo have shown that each and every rainforest tree supports about one thousand insect species. One of the strangest inhabitants of the rainforest is the stalk-eyed fly. This fly has very large eyestalks that project out of the side of its head. Females of the species always choose to mate with the fly that has the longer eyestalk. The whip scorpion has a leathery hard upper shell and a long whip-like tail. When it is frightened it sprays a strong, foul-smelling chemical at its attacker. It is very good at controlling the cockroach population in the jungle.

Insect Diversity in the Amazon Rainforest with Terry Erwin – Terry Erwin is an expert on insect diversity and talks about his studies of insects in the Amazon rainforest.

CHAPTER 11

Deforestation

The current deforestation rate is estimated to be one acre every second (a piece of land about the size of a football field). That means sixty acres each minute, 3,600 acres every hour, 86,400 acres each day, 2.6 million acres each month, and 31.5 million acres of rainforest is being destroyed each year.

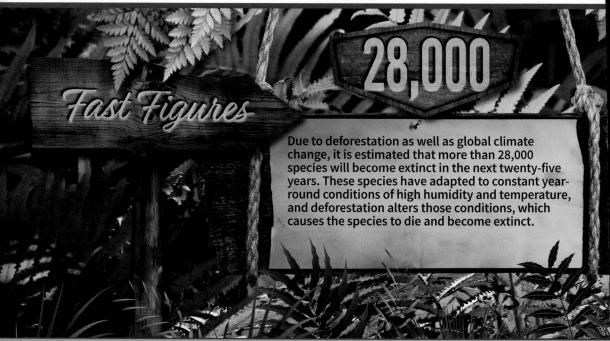

Fast Figures

28,000

Due to deforestation as well as global climate change, it is estimated that more than 28,000 species will become extinct in the next twenty-five years. These species have adapted to constant year-round conditions of high humidity and temperature, and deforestation alters those conditions, which causes the species to die and become extinct.

Sometimes jungles are burned deliberately to make charcoal or clear land for agriculture.

8%

Currently, 8% of Sarawak rainforest land consists of "protected reserves." However, these areas are understaffed, and illegal logging still continues inside their borders. Also, colonists continue to move in illegally and make settlements near remote logging roads.

80-90

Currently, 6% of the world is rainforest. If deforestation continues at its present rate, there won't be any rainforests left in the world in 80–90 years.

The jungle is cleared daily for large-scale cattle ranching, logging timber, mining and military operations, hydroelectric plants, government road building, and large industrial farming, as well as for small farms for landless settlers. Parts of rainforests are even being burned to make charcoal to provide power for industrial plants. What are the effects of massive deforestation? There are many ugly consequences—soil erosion, water and air pollution, excessive carbon dioxide released into the atmosphere, the eviction and death of native indigenous tribes, and biodiversity loss caused by the extinction of animals and plants. Worst of all, the rainforests of the world could disappear completely in less than a century.

SARAWAK, BORNEO RAINFOREST DEFORESTATION

The jungles of Borneo underwent such drastic deforestation in the 80s and 90s, achieved by burning, logging, and clearing, that the rate of destruction has no parallel in human history. The rainforest land was changed into palm oil plantations and agricultural land. Excessive logging was done to supply both the Malaysian and world plywood industry. Although indigenous people managed to slow down the destruction by attracting some attention to the plight of the rainforest through peaceful demonstrations and contacting environmental activists, it still continues today.

PAPUA NEW GUINEA RAINFOREST DEFORESTATION

Deforestation in Papua New Guinea is extensive and is caused primarily by illegal logging, which makes up 70%–90% of timber exports from the country. Studies by environmental organizations have shown that this great rate of illegal logging is tied to political corruption, which causes harsh oppression and punishment of local workers and anyone who dares to question the legality of the loggers. A law was passed in 2010 that took away the rights of all indigenous people to question any decisions concerning the country's natural resources.

CONGO RAINFOREST DEFORESTATION

Deforestation in the Congo has remained steady since 1990, with 1,200 square miles of forest being lost annually. The loss of jungle habitat causes soil erosion, decreased biodiversity, climate change, and a loss of habitat for mountain gorillas, okapi, and other rare species. The main causes of deforestation are road development, the collection of charcoal and fuelwood, small-scale logging, and slashing and burning of the forests for transformation into farmland.

In Brazil, creating space for cattle ranching is responsible for eighty percent of that country's deforestation.

AMAZON RAINFOREST DEFORESTATION

The time of greatest forest loss in the Amazon rainforest was from 1991–2004, with periods of increased loss in 2008 and 2013. Eighty percent of the deforestation is due to the Brazilian cattle traders who make their fortunes by selling beef and leather worldwide from animals that have been raised on farmland that used to be rainforest. Other destroyers of the jungle are loggers, large-scale farming operations of palm, soy, and other crops, and small-scale farmers. Research has shown that the more rainforest that is destroyed means the less rain that reaches the area, making the cleared land less suitable for farming purposes.

The Borneo Rainforest – This beautiful video features an interesting and informative introduction to the Borneo Rainforest.

CHAPTER 12

Making a Difference: Foundations to Save the Rainforests

AMAZON REGION (ARPA)

Brazil began the fight to conserve the Amazon rainforest in 2002 when it created Amazon Region Protected Areas (ARPA). The goal was to transform 150 million acres of the Amazon rainforest that lie in Brazil into smaller areas of sustainable use and to strictly protect other areas. In ten years this group, working together with the Brazilian government and the WWF (World Wildlife Fund), managed to protect a portion of the jungle that is as large as the state of California. They are currently working on ARPA For Life, which will use a fund of $215 million collected from around the world to help pay the government of Brazil to fully maintain the portion of the rainforest that they have preserved.

COOL EARTH

Cool Earth is a non-profit organization that is working with rainforest communities in the Amazon, Borneo, Congo, and Papua New Guinea to stop climate change and deforestation. They work to support and educate the indigenous people who live in or near the rainforests and help to find them new jobs that don't involve working with outside corporations who pay them low wages to help cut down all the trees in the jungle.

Cool Earth uses satellite imagery to keep watch over the rainforests to make sure that the canopy cover of the forest is not disappearing. They put camera traps and laptops inside the jungle to share and monitor the latest images of what is happening in the rainforest. They also use these cameras to capture images of the wildlife that we have never been able to see up close. They've taken pictures of the rare Peruvian spectacled bear and the forest bittern and southern crowned pigeon in Papua New

Fast Figures

3

Coalition For Rainforest Nations consists of members from countries that have tropical forests that are interested in working collaboratively to responsibly balance care of the forests and economic development. They have collected more than $3 billion from industrialized countries to work to reduce the rate of deforestation in the rainforests.

Guinea that thrill the people who live so close to them.

As of February 2018, Cool Earth has saved 901,679 acres of rainforest, protected 216,402,960 trees, saved 68,527,604,00 liters of water, and has helped to store 234,436,540 tons of carbon dioxide.

WWF (WORLD WILDLIFE FUND)

WWF was started on April 29, 1961, to combat deforestation, climate change, and threats to wildlife and all wild places around the world. They are now the Earth's biggest and most successful independent conservation organization. WWF has worked for forty years in the Amazon Basin to protect the jungle; enhancing the conservation of wildlife, plants, and trees; and reducing human impact in all of its many forms (logging, burning down the jungle to create farms, etc.). In the rainforests of Papua New Guinea, WWF has made six tree kangaroo species a priority by making sure that their habitat is not destroyed. In Borneo,

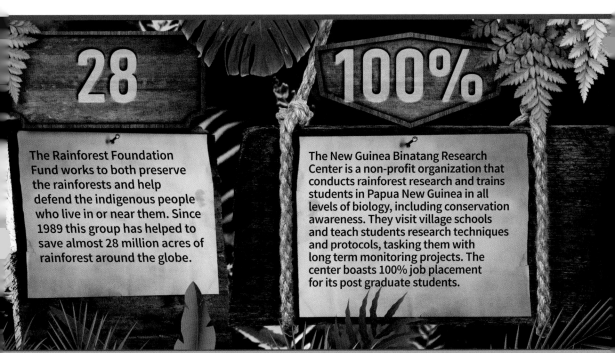

28

The Rainforest Foundation Fund works to both preserve the rainforests and help defend the indigenous people who live in or near them. Since 1989 this group has helped to save almost 28 million acres of rainforest around the globe.

100%

The New Guinea Binatang Research Center is a non-profit organization that conducts rainforest research and trains students in Papua New Guinea in all levels of biology, including conservation awareness. They visit village schools and teach students research techniques and protocols, tasking them with long term monitoring projects. The center boasts 100% job placement for its post graduate students.

the WWF has worked for many years to limit mining and logging in the rainforest, protect orangutans and all other native wildlife species, stop illegal hunting, and fight against the threat of enormous oil palm plantations. WWF has also fought tirelessly to protect the Congo Basin and all its animals and plant species.

The World Wildlife Fund is one of several groups that work to protect the Amazon rainforest from being cut down.

RAINFOREST RESCUE

Since 1986, the nonprofit Australian organization Rainforest Rescue has been interfering with the financial interests of mining, oil, cattle and timber companies, corrupt politicians, and banks that want to make large profits from destroying rainforests around the world, while at the same time robbing indigenous tribes, small farmers and rubber tappers of their jobs and livelihood. Rainforest Rescue raises funds to buy rainforest property and fight large corporations in court. They work closely with Save Our Borneo, an environmental organization that is carrying on a battle with the destroyers of the jungle there in Borneo, and DECOIN, a group in Ecuador that is fighting relentlessly to protect unique rainforest species in the Amazon.

WORLD LAND TRUST

WLT (World Land Trust), an organization in the United Kingdom, has worked without stopping for more than twenty-five years to restore degraded habitats and create new and protected nature reserves in the world's rainforests. They acquire threatened land, provide funds for tree planting to restore land that has been deforested and work with other groups to reduce forest degradation and emissions caused by deforestation. All of their projects are managed by local organizations.

AMAZON WATCH

Amazon Watch is an organization that works to help the 250,000 human inhabitants of the Amazon jungle with their needs. These indigenous people, who belong to 215 different ethnic groups and speak more than 170 different languages, have been taken advantage of and even killed by government groups and corporations who want to take away all the land and use the rainforest for quick profits. Amazon Watch helps these people to fight against the groups that want to hurt them by hiring lawyers to fight for them in courts, calling for corporate accountability, and working together with environmental organizations to preserve the Amazon rainforest.

Rainforest Rescue Daintree Rainforest – This video was created by the very successful Daintree Buy Back and Protect Forever project which identifies and then buys rainforests around the world that are at risk of development.

SERIES GLOSSARY OF KEY TERMS

Assimilation - the process by which a person or persons acquire the social and psychological characteristics of a group or society

Canopy - also called crown canopy or crown cover, this refers to the cover formed by the leafy upper branches of the trees in a forest

Carnivorous - subsisting or feeding on animal tissues, or in the case of some plants, subsisting on nutrients obtained from the breakdown of animal protoplasm

Colonialism - control by one country over another area and its people

Conservation - a careful preservation and protection of something, such as the planned management of a natural resource to prevent exploitation, destruction, or neglect

Creature – an animal of any type

Culture – the customary beliefs, social forms, and material traits of a racial, religious, or social group, and the characteristic features of everyday existence (such as diversions or a way of life) shared by the people of those groups in a place or time

Deforestation – the action or process of the clearing of forests through cutting or burning its trees

Enzymes - any of numerous complex proteins that are produced by living cells and catalyze specific natural biochemical reactions at body temperatures, such as digestion

Habitat - the place or environment where a plant or animal naturally or normally lives and grows

Indigenous - produced, growing, living, or occurring naturally in a particular region or environment

Nocturnal - active at night

Oxygen - a reactive element that is found in water, in most rocks and minerals, in numerous organic compounds, and as a colorless tasteless odorless diatomic gas constituting 21 percent of the atmosphere, that is capable of combining with all elements except the inert gases and is active in physio-logical processes; estimates say that trees of the world's jungles produce 30 to 55 percent of the oxygen in the atmosphere

Parasite - an animal, insect or plant that lives in or on another animal or plant and gets food or protection from it

Poaching – to trespass on land for the purpose of taking fish or game illegally

Predator - an animal that lives by killing and eating other animals

Rainforest - a tropical woodland with an annual rainfall of at least 100 inches (254 centimeters) and marked by lofty broad-leaved evergreen trees forming a continuous canopy

Species - a category of biological classification ranking immediately below the genus or subgenus, comprising related organisms or populations potentially capable of inter-breeding, and being designated by a common name

Tropical - of, being, or characteristic of a region or climate that is frost-free with temperatures high enough to support year-round plant growth given sufficient moisture

Venom - a toxic substance produced by some animals (such as snakes, scorpions, or bees) that is injected into prey or an enemy chiefly by biting or stinging and has an injurious or lethal effect

DOCUMENTARIES

The Jungle of the Red Spirit, 2012

The jungles of Borneo are especially famous for the enormous number of species of the most sophisticated flower in the world—the Orchid. In this documentary, viewers will see the beauty close-up as they climb the tree trunks of this beautiful jungle guided by the "man of the forest."

The Sacred Science, 2011

In October of 2010, eight people, suffering from various illnesses, chose to leave everything behind and spend thirty days in a corner of the world that is home to a vanishing group of indigenous healers in uncharted regions of the Amazon rainforest. Five would come back with real results, two would come back disappointed, and one wouldn't come back at all. This is their story.

Swamp Tigers, 2001

This documentary takes a look at one of the most efficient predators on Earth. Cameraman Mike Herd captured the legendary swamp tiger on film for the first time years ago. It was an extraordinary breakthrough, the first glimpse into the secret life of the least known tiger in the world - the swamp tiger of the Bangladeshi Sundarbans.

RESOURCES

Further Reading

Barker, John. *Ancestral Lines: The Maisin of Papua New Guinea and the Fate of the Rainforest* (2nd ed.). Toronto: University of Toronto Press, Higher Education Division, 2007.

Magdalena, Carlos. *The Plant Messiah: Adventures in Search of the World's Rarest Species.* New York, NY: Viking Press, 2017.

Newman, Arnold. *The Tropical Rainforest: A World Survey of Our Most Valuable Endangered Habitat: With a Blueprint for Its Survival.* New York, NY: Checkmark Books, 2000.

Preston, Douglas. *The Lost City of The Monkey God: A True Story.* New York, NY: Grand Central Publishing, 2017.

Straumann, Lukas. *Money Logging: On the Trail of the Asian Timber Mafia.* Basel, Switzerland: Bergli Books, 2014.

Taylor, Leslie. *The Healing Power of Rainforest Herbs: A Guide to Understanding and Using Herbal Medicines.* New Hyde Park, NY: Square One Publishers, 2005.

Woolf, Alex. *Trekking in the Congo Rainforest.* Buffalo, NY: Gareth Stevens Publishing, 2013.

Internet Resources

https://www.conserve-energy-future.com/tropical-rainforest-biome.php

Conserve Energy Future provides an interesting overview of the animals, plants, location, climate, and temperature of the world's largest rainforests.

https://www.rainforest-alliance.org/

Rainforest Alliance (an international nonprofit organization) has a long track record of working for the conservation of rainforest biodiversity as well as sustainable livelihoods of the people who live in and around the rainforest.

https://www.rainforestmaker.org

Rainforest Maker provides many facts concerning rainforests, as well as links to local projects that allow students to become involved with efforts to conserve the environment.

http://w3.marietta.edu/~biol/biomes/troprain.htm

Tropical Rain Forest. This is an excellent webpage with many photos taken during visits to rainforests by Marietta College's Program of Biology and Environmental Science.

https://www.tropical-rainforest-animals.com/

The Tropical Rainforest Animals website provides statistics and information on endangered rainforest animals, plus rainforest destruction, articles on environmental pollution, and articles on the rainforests in the Amazon and in Borneo.

Educational Video Links

Chapter 1: http://x-qr.net/1DP7

Learn about the modern-day search for the ancient lost city of the monkey god in Honduras.

Chapter 2: http://x-qr.net/1D5b

This video contains some amazing facts about the jungles of the Amazon Basin.

Chapter 3: http://x-qr.net/1GYr

Diana Rios is a member of the Ashéninka tribe of Saweto, Peru. After her father and other community leaders were murdered, Diana took over their role as defender of the rainforest.

Chapter 4: http://x-qr.net/1Hoo

Justin Catanoso is an expert on climate change and has won a Pulitzer Prize for his coverage of the topic.

Chapter 5: http://x-qr.net/1FFp

This fascinating video shows Kendalyn Hersh, a Radford University student, teach a group of visitors about the value of Amazonian medicinal plants.

Chapter 6: http://x-qr.net/1DkG

This lighthearted video clearly explains some facts about both tropical and temperate rainforest ecosystems.

Chapter 7: http://x-qr.net/1DKh

A well done school project concerning endangered Amazon region species.

Chapter 8: http://x-qr.net/1Hij

A good introductory video demonstrating some of the many products that come from rainforests.

Chapter 9: http://x-qr.net/1F1n

This is a good introductory video about the diversity of tropical rainforests created by the California Academy of Sciences.

Chapter 10: http://x-qr.net/1DBv

Terry Erwin is an expert on insect diversity and talks about his studies of insects in the Amazon rainforest.

Chapter 11: http://x-qr.net/1GWj

This beautiful video features an interesting and informative introduction to the Borneo Rainforest.

Chapter 12: http://x-qr.net/1E1Q

This very well done video was created by a student and clearly explains the different layers of the rainforest.

INDEX

political corruption, 62–63, 68
pollution, Congo rainforests, 43
preservation, 9
products from the rainforests, 45–49
Puncak Jaya (New Guinea), 16

ABOUT THE AUTHOR

Lori is a graduate of the University of Pittsburgh and has traveled all over Central and South America. She loves books, learning, music, traveling, and new opportunities. Since an early age, she has written articles for newspapers and magazines. For more than a decade, she has been an editorial and design judge for the Benjamin Franklin Publishing Awards. As a cataloger in a large university library, she created thousands of bibliographic records detailing content and subject headings of books. She is also a prolific blogger known for her thoughtful writing, as well as her keen sense of humor. To top it all off, Lori is fluent in Spanish.